I WISHED

ALSO BY DENNIS COOPER

The George Miles Cycle

Closer

Frisk

Try

Guide

Period

Other Fiction

Wrong

My Loose Thread

The Sluts

God Jr.

Ugly Man

The Marbled Swarm

I
WISHED

DENNIS
COOPER

SOHO

Published by
Soho Press, Inc.
227 W 17th Street
New York, NY 10011

Library of Congress Cataloging-in-Publication Data

Names: Cooper, Dennis, 1953- author.
Title: I wished / Dennis Cooper.
Description: New York, NY : Soho, [2021]
Identifiers: LCCN 2021011525

ISBN 978-1-64129-304-4
eISBN 978-1-64129-305-1

Classification: LCC PS3553.O582 I24 2021 | DDC 813/.54—dc23
LC record available at https://lccn.loc.gov/2021011525

Interior design by Janine Agro, Soho Press, Inc.

Printed in the United States of America

10 9 8 7 6 5 4 3 2 1

for Zac Farley

I WISHED

OVERTURE
(2021)

I started writing books about and for my friend George Miles because whenever I would speak about him honestly like I am doing now I felt a complicated agony beneath my words that talking openly can't handle.

There's no one I can talk to, basically. Every friend I used to have who also knew him hasn't sought me out in years, which would be easy since I'm very mildly famous, whereas their last names are so commonplace that, when I search the web for them, literally thousands of candidates show up.

I've talked about my friend in so many articles and interviews. If you do a search using his name, pages and pages will turn up, and every one that's not about some far-flung namesake is either by me or about me, or it's something made by someone who only knows the characters I've named for him.

How could someone like him die without a single friend or member of his family ever putting up a tribute page or even mentioning his name in tweets or Facebook posts, even on his birthday or on his death day's anniversary or even randomly in reference to something in their lives or art that brought his memory to mind.

Why hasn't anyone who knew him ever tried to contact me to say, "I knew him too," or "Thank you for devoting so much writing to him," or "How could you have written such disturbing things about my friend or brother or former boyfriend or son or cousin?" Is what I've done that obscure? I guess.

When George doesn't cross my mind, which can happen for a while, weeks, months, I'm okay, but then I think of him and get like this. But not "like this" because I almost never talk about him, period. I'll say a little, and people will say, "That's interesting and sad." But they mean for me and not for him.

Or I write about him, and my readers say, "That's sick or awesome, or he's so cute, or he's too unsympathetic, or he's very touching, or he's boring, or he's really sexy, or I knew someone like him too, or I relate to him so much," which is the best or only meaningful response that I can even hope for. That's as good as it will ever get for him.

I saw a therapist for three years, and I talked about him there, but she said he was a symbol in my lifelong playing out of shit my parents did to me, and she just wanted me to talk about my past, not him. I would ask her please, please forget about me and think of me as just some person who is telling you about him.

I know how difficult he was to be around, and how emotionally hot and cold, and I understand he did and said some awful things to people near the end when I wasn't with him unforgivably, but could his death really have been such a big relief to everyone? Like, I never need to think about that guy again?

I had a friend who claims to be a psychic. She did a reading for me once and said she saw him hovering above my head or something. She said he's always watching over me, feeling so much love and gratitude for something that I used to do for him or have been doing since he died, and I almost believed her, and maybe I even do. That's how easy it is to hurt me.

Even now I think, What if her envisioning was true, because I want so unbelievably and inexpressibly for him to know he meant and means so much to me that I have written and still keep writing all these elegies and things, even when I'm not communicating anything beyond my need to talk about him, but why?

I guess because I want someone who knew my friend to read this book and find me. I want this book to be more public than my others so it will find people who don't normally read novels or who don't give a shit about some weird cult writer's books because it seems like everyone who either knew him or used to know me doesn't.

I want to know that all my love for him is worth it or find someone who'll convince me he was no one much, or who'll say, "He never mentioned you," or that he referenced me offhandedly enough that it's clear I didn't mean that much to him, and that's the hope, and that's the fear, and I know that's only semi-interesting to read, but it's very hard for me to even do this.

TORN FROM
SOMETHING

George's father is a failed Olympic gymnast who seems overly stand-offish and dejected even for a Russian. He still looks teenaged in his early 30s except when he takes off his shirt, because there's something too dog-eared about his muscles. George thinks he'd look exactly like his father if his father were a worm. He's a 12-year-old nobody much who wishes he could play guitar and is watching an American cartoon.

Every country dubs its language over foreigners' TV shows, but in Russia it's a racket. One sermonizing voice reads the actors' dialogue as though the show were an appliance and their gab were its instructions while the real, sweet noises rollick faintly in the background. That's how the rest of the world sounds to Russians if they pay any attention at all.

Donald Duck and his preposterous cohorts are like dolphins signaling their happiness to Russians through a bleak, indifferent surface. It's a form of mind control that dates back to when the Communists ran everything and makes children of an introspective bent think they can hear the truth attacking through their fruity little thoughts.

George is chuckling at the TV's muffled playthings and hoping his mother will stand up. His father was scrubbing their bedroom furniture and walls with her fighting, flopping body for a long time. That sounded too familiar, but not the silence afterward that will not stop. George's mind is saying, If your mother's dead, you'd better kill yourself.

George's father barges in the living room and sits bizarrely near his son, which he'd never thought to try before. He seems dazed by the unprecedented access, and his hands throb from having finally killed his wife.

He knows he'll have to kill George now, but first he tries watching the cartoons' rat-a-tatting nonsense.

George isn't old enough to be a loss. He'll just turn one dead body into two, which isn't very different. People in their building have heard him beat his wife and son so many times they must be numbed. Maybe he could rape George if he finally wants to. Would those screams sound inconsistent? The only danger is he might kill himself for doing that. Is that a problem?

When George's father was an 8-year-old, investigators from the agency of sports made a routine visit to his school. After watching him cartwheel and twirl above the playground's swings and jungle gym, they bought him from his parents. He was positioned in a prison-like academy for potential medal winners along with close to 40 other boys with magic bodies.

He was trained to win gold medals in gymnastics with short daily morning breaks to add a barren education. Sometimes he contested in minor showcase competitions in far-flung Russian provinces. He never won anything, but the crowds were full of pedophiles and girls who liked the prettiest contestant, and that was him.

So many film crews shot George's father's grimacing, angelic face that it became the public's mental image of Russia's gymnastics might for years. That usefulness kept him in the running long after better gymnasts had been axed. Nowadays, when people see George's father on the street, they often ask if he looked younger and important once.

George's father unties his shoes and shakes them loose. He whips his T-shirt off. He unzips his pants, or starts to. He rises to his feet so he can slide them down, but he's infirm from having killed his wife and so much less attracted to the chance of winning something that he slumps back on the couch instead and rubs his sore hands together.

He starts to push George's head into his crotch, but the head feels like a lightly garnished skull. It makes him stop and think about the brain inside and then his son's dumb thoughts, whatever they might be. He pets the head while envisaging the thoughts he'd like to work with and then, having made George game, lifts his hand off like a starting gate.

George looks up weirdly at his father, then removes his T-shirt too. He holds the T-shirt tensely in his hand. George's father rips it from his son's hand and holds it stiffly in his own. He gives it half a chance to be a shirt, then thinks the Russian equivalent of "fuck it" and wads the cloth until it's flower-shaped, then sniffs the image.

His erection's coarse, straightforward wish gets dubbed atop whatever happiness his son and he had made together. He sort of wants to give the flower to George, but love seems stupid, so he drops the shirt, then makes a fist instead. George takes a giant breath, then arcs his back to make the strongest chest his rib cage can create.

"Why did you take off your shirt?" George's father asks.

"Because you did," George says.

"Aren't you scared?" George's father asks.

George nervously unlocks the tongue and buckle of his belt, which has a cowboy style. "Yes," he says.

George's father puts one hand inside the flash of underwear and grabs.

"It says yes too," he says.

"It probably thinks your hand is mine," George says.

"Do you jack off?" George's father asks.

"Sometimes," George says.

"What do you think about when you jack off?" George's father asks.

"What's the right answer?" George asks. He looks into his father's eyes, which either don't mean shit or are outdistanced by his mind's scared shit, then thinks about the question. "Sometimes my mother."

"Your mother doing what?" George's father asks and starts jacking off his son, who winces.

"Not this," George says. "You should lick your fingers first."

One of George's bandmates is a fried, revered guitarist who still picks out flabbergasting notes, but they're strange now. George thinks he'd play guitar remotely like his bandmate if his bandmate were a drunk. He's a skinny 16-year-old prodigy from Brixton drinking gin and watching dead guitarists play the blues with old acoustic instruments on some TV thing.

Every older era's sense of scale and vintage tech turn off the young, but to radicals like George, it's especially deterring. Between the dead guitarists' minor outreach and the distanced, scratchy footage, they might as well be fiddling with loaded rifles that'll only hurt themselves. That's how other people's sadness sounds to George when he cares at all.

The blues' originators could be dolphins signaling their primitive unhappiness to more experimental artists. The fact that even innovative art grows cordial over time is a catastrophe that makes groundbreaking young musicians with drinking problems for good reasons know they can't be gods with giant amps despite the bliss that animates them when they're trying hard.

George is playing his unplugged Strat with the TV's ghosts and hoping his bandmate hasn't quit their band despite the recent hellishness of being with him. He and other members had been yelling one another in the background for a long time. That sounded usual of late, but not the silence ever since that will not stop. George's mind is saying, "If my bandmate quit, I'm dead."

George's bandmate joins him on the couch and sits unnaturally close. He's never longed to be right next to George until right now, and it's disorienting to be pressed against someone he only hugs onstage in acts of showmanship, and his dilated eyes are wet from having quit their band. He knows he needs to say goodbye, but first he tries watching the TV.

George isn't bold enough to be the leader of the band or play the notes alone without lessening their vistas. If the band breaks up, there'll just be two casualties instead of one. Their fans aren't smart enough to understand their genius anyway, so would George's lack of daring even sound that different? Still, George would know. Is that a problem?

George's bandmate used to play guitar in shitty local bands as though they mattered. The leader of a critically anointed band that played electric blues observed him bend strings incongruously and fit him in their higher ranks. George's bandmate gigged and played on albums with this band until their orthodoxy started to feel dumbass and claustrophobic.

He started his own band that used the blues as roots not a criterion. He came across a 15-year-old George playing wildly with a local band and hired the boy to be their novelty. Their complicated grittiness exhilarated critics, which ushered in the public, who didn't understand a thing but lied so they could gawk at George, who looked 13 years old if anything.

But George's bandmate wanted to rewire the way sound whistles through guitars, which needed psychedelic drugs, he thought. George needed to destroy something inside himself that no one else could understand to play at all, and alcohol helped. Their problems worked artistically, but George's bandmate went insane, and George's playing stalled, and now it's all fucked up and over.

George's bandmate watches him exaggerate the notes that legends play so simply in the past. He doesn't know if he's too fried to judge the difference anymore, but even on a muted Strat, there's something cold in George's tone that, say, the legends just unleash into their music like hysteria. This so depresses George's bandmate that he wants to join the band again but doesn't.

He tries stroking George's head in hopes that, with the help of psychedelic drugs, he'll somehow feel what's going wrong inside a brain so young yet status quo. He can't, and George tenses at the touch, which makes his playing worse, which makes him stop and drink instead. So George's bandmate borrows the guitar and plays the licks.

George drinks. Even six weeks back, he would have learned something or thought he had from studying his bandmate's outré fingering and hazardous decisions. He might have taken the guitar and tried to top him, and their band would peak. This difference kills him, so he grabs the instrument away, then throws it at the TV set but nothing breaks.

So, that's that, the band is over, even if, when George's bandmate plays sans George in the future—if, that is, he doesn't drug himself into a state where music sounds too idiotic—it could expose his young friend's insufficiencies and so detach his risky notes from the cohesion George's playing lent them that he'll just end up scribbling obscure crap.

· · ·

"Why did you do that," asks George's bandmate. He's on his feet retrieving the Strat from where it struck the floor. Now he sits down again already playing it.

"Because you quit," George says.

"You're not inside yourself," says George's bandmate. He tries to twist his guilt into an interstellar note.

"Is that it?" George asks.

"I know I'll sound like I'm a barking dog, but I love you," says George's bandmate.

"So, don't quit," George says so flatly that he knows he really means it.

"Do you still believe in reinventing sound?" asks George's bandmate. By now, his soloing has edged into a string of noise.

"Sometimes," George says.

"What do you think about when you believe that?" asks George's bandmate.

"Usually you," George says.

"Me doing what?" George's bandmate says. By now, he's playing notes that don't connect and make no sense at all.

"Not this," George says and blunts the fret-board with his hand. "Not this crazy motherfucking sounding shit that makes me feel so lost."

· · ·

Whomsoever George is chatting with types or thinks as raucously as he does. To guess, they're in their teens or early 20s—two needy losers or ironic raconteurs using punctuation marks and letters on their keyboards like little shovels as though the English language is a bunch of dirt so they'll sound as convoluted as they really are.

Every website's chat room hauls in lonesome people editing their vibes into emoticons and cramping up their sentences, but the site George frequents is for maniacs. To visitors, it might appear as though a bunch of suicidal people are transcribing some collective, self-inflicted shootout wherein the typos are escaping bits of shrapnel, but for them it's more like finger painting.

George is like a dolphin flagging humans from beneath articulation's choppy surface. It's a form of operatic laziness about the rules of composition dating back to when the Internet freed every word that has eroded or been tortured over time into a jewel-like, pleading noise that helps George blurt and cry in public without losing his composure.

He's slopping out his tumult while trying to detect if any other fumbling chatters are upset because of him, and he may have isolated one. There's just the trace of intake in the guy's harangue—dents or dings or maybe even wounds as codependent as those calling and responding bleats that saxophonists traded in the jazz records his father played incessantly.

If all the chatters, George included, were just segments in a kind of typist choir, each performing a distinctive tonal fraction of some abrasive score, then . . . That's too difficult to imagine being true, so . . . maybe if their heated ramblings are just linguistic shreds dispensing outward from some disco ball–like application embedded in the website, which could possibly be true, then . . .

If the garbage in their voices could be scraped away, maybe they're intelligent or draw less stupid pictures or are prettier or something great that some vindictive, lesser mortals have so teased or criticized into seclusion that they're only true when fighting one another for attention with a font's cache of modifiers as their weaponry.

Maybe when they're not online, they shadow colleges' or high schools' walls. Maybe they're goths or emos who have gussied up life's hellishness into a daily Halloween. Maybe their trendiness solved people's meanness into an issue of conflicting tastes in fashion, which hurts less but makes it extremely difficult for them to make close friends.

Maybe they write poetry about their feelings and

read that to one another while imagining their listeners are attachés or scouts from lyrically impaired but otherwise amazing bands. Maybe no one actually listens, they just wait their turn to read, and vice versa, so they don't know why they feel comfortable yet miserably alone when they're together.

Maybe they grew bold enough one day to post their poems on websites set aside for gloomy, unsophisticated artists and admirers of incompetent, cathartic art. Maybe they grew confident enough to stop pretending their scribbles were poetry instead of suicidal scrawls they might have chickened out and torn in shreds were not the Internet a wildly more rewarding trash can.

Maybe someone loved them once or twice, or said they did, which they no more believed than actors buy the love of fans that only know them when their feelings are impersonations. So, love got lost, and now that they're so doomed, or wish they were, they know that mutual addiction will have to do, and they're trying to addict someone right now.

At some point, George's chat-mate hints it might be safe to switch on their respective webcams and illuminate their separate cockpits, and George, gambling that the correlations in their ranting back and forth will make his chat-mate's face a witching mirror image, types okay amongst a burst of words about his less than magical appearance.

George is startled that his chat-mate is a little boy, maybe 12 years old at most. He's sitting in a brightly daylit room with posters of some athlete on the walls, and he looks strangely tickled that George is old enough to be his father and lives far enough away from him that, judging by a wall clock in the background, it's the middle of the night there.

"My English . . . you already know it is very bad," the boy says in some thick and somber accent. He leans into his desktop to study George, who sees some bruises on his face.

"I thought you were faking it like I was," George says.

"No," the boy says. "I try to write very hard."

"So . . . why are you fucked up?" George asks.

"Because my father killed my mother," the boy says. He leans back and looks away and starts to cry. "And . . . now he's raping me sometimes."

"I wish I could do something to help," George says. "But it looks like you live very far away."

The boy gives George a careful glance. "Why are you sad?" he asks.

"Because . . . God, so many reasons," George says. "I've been bipolar all my life, and now it's gotten even worse, and they're saying I'm psychotic."

"I want to kill myself," the boy says.

"You shouldn't," George says. He mumbles "shit" under his breath and tenses up and moves his cursor to the spot where he can shut the application with a tap. "You'll hurt someone. Hurting other people is the only reason I don't do it."

"No, just me," the boy says. "No one cares. I—"

"Look," George says, "if you'd told me this when we were chatting, I might have thought, Whatever, I don't know this guy, maybe he's lying, but . . . you're a little kid, and . . . I can't let you hurt me."

"I won't hurt you," the boy says. He grabs his face and sobs and starts to shout things in some other language, and it's so frightening that George could make some little kid he barely even knows feel this horrible.

George's high school friend is still his best although they haven't talked in years and live half a world apart. George had planned to move away from home but never did or barely even. He thinks he'd live in France if there had been a genius medication. He's a 30-year-old failed musician with severe bipolar illness holding a loaded gun and listening to Nick Drake late at night.

Everyone who loves Drake thinks they share what made his early records sound so sad, then grow so bleak, but George extremely does. Maybe if he had unleashed his pain artistically he would feel different, but for now it's like Drake's lyrics are his thoughts after being edited and scored by someone just like him but more important.

Nick Drake's songs are like a pack of dolphins signaling his solitude incoherently to George and other introverted messes. It's a very tight relationship between suicidal artists and their suicidal listeners that has been curing or killing guys like Drake and George forever. When everyone you know is either very far away from you or hides, you find someone dead to love.

George is holding the gun like it's a phone and wishing his old friend would somehow call him. His friend wrote him letters for a while, but George would never write him back, not even when he moved and got a new address, and now he's moved so many times the letters couldn't be forwarded to him if they were magic, and George's phone is just a gun.

According to some article, Nick Drake grew so sad he had to move in with his parents. Every day he left their home and walked to an abandoned house, then sat down on the floor where local junkies gathered daily to shootup, then die or not. He wouldn't do their drugs or talk to anyone, and none of them knew why he came or stayed or who he was or ever acted like they cared.

Maybe he admired their love of almost dying. Maybe he was studying the painless things they said when they were almost dead. Maybe they spoke for him just like his music does for George. Maybe they enjoyed the company or pitied him and thought, "At least we have this drug, and imagine if we didn't." Then he would leave, and they would say, "That guy is weird," no matter what they felt.

Years later, a journalist learned where Nick Drake died and somehow met one of those junkies, who recognized Drake's photo. He said Drake came and went for months. They'd only let him stay because one of the junkie girls thought he was handsome. The last time, just before he left, he'd started crying, and, when they heard and looked, he said, "You guys know me. Tell me what is wrong with me."

When George's best friend was 15, they met. George fell in love so fast his parents thought it was a gay thing. It wasn't, even though George wanted it to be, but he was 12. For him, it felt like being a magician's trick. He snuck around and lied about his whereabouts so they could be alone and talk. His other friends thought that was odd, but no one understood why George did anything.

Even as a kid, George stayed upset too lengthily and acted too revved up by friends and things he liked, but he was cute, which made the fluctuating mostly fun for everyone until he worsened. By 14, he would either not shut up or stared at friends like they were walls, and almost everyone he knew decided they'd had crushes on him that they'd now outgrown.

By 15, George would stay in bed for weeks. His best friend sat with him sometimes, and it was rough, but at least they were alone like George had wanted. Even his parents, who'd tried to exile George's friend, said, "Be our guest." Up until his late teens, George would sometimes find a drug or some belief or girlfriend, and he would tell his friend, I need to love myself or God or her or anyone but you.

He found an almost genius medication at 18, but its side effects made him so horny that love turned into an offshoot from his crotch. His problems grew as simple as the gap between his body and his friend's. They started fucking, which made their love deducible at last and look completely normal from the outside.

But then the pill stopped working, tearing George in half again.

One day his best friend said, "If I haven't worked for you by now, I think I won't." He decided he was free to move across the world and be an artist. George tried to be an artist but was too fucked up to give his pain a surface. He found a girlfriend who got sick of his insanity. When she dumped him, he threatened her and was arrested. He agreed to move in with his parents to avoid a trial. The phone rings.

"Why did you love me?" George asks whoever's calling him.

"Because you love me so much," says the voice.

"But I don't," George says. "If I did I wouldn't do what I'm about to."

"I swear to God you do," says the voice.

"What about when I was manic?" George asks.

"I pretended you were giving me a standing ovation," says the voice.

"And when I was catatonic?" George asks.

"I would look at you and fantasize," says the voice.

"I'm sorry that I never . . ." George starts to say into the phone, or, rather, to the phone since no one's there, and not actually to a phone since what he's holding to his head is just the gun. He never finishes the sentence, because he isn't sorry.

"What's that music in the background?" asks the voice. "It's beautiful."

"If you love me, you'll hang up now," George says. He thinks the caller would hang up then. He makes that happen even though it hurts. He knows it's real because he hears the click.

THIALH

When I was 17, I planned to write a novel that would somehow ply and individualize *The Heart Is a Lonely Hunter*. Not the Carson McCullers book, which I'd maybe read with no effect in junior high school, but the lesser-known filmed version. It starred Alan Arkin and was probably released in the later 1960s, but I've decided not to fact-check what I'm writing since the movie's less the architecture of my thoughts than their brunt. In any case, the movie must have bombed, since, by the time I'd finally gained the chops to maybe write my version, no one I knew had even heard of it.

I was in my middle-20s then, and the movie's details were erased, or largely so, like preliminary pencil marks or powers of suggestion whose only purpose was to float a revelation I'd experienced while watching it. I rarely cry, even when alone, but I did, and with an unusual lack of self-control, blubbering right there amongst the movie's other, less absorbed customers. I continued to cry off and on for days afterward because, as best I can remember, Alan Arkin's character seemed to me a kind of distillation of what was deeply wrong with me.

In my reckless memory, there was something physically screwed up with Arkin's character, whose "name" I can't remember anymore, and who I've decided might as well have had my name, which is Dennis. Maybe Dennis was blind or deaf. Those are my guesses. But he was very kind and generous, or else he had become innately kind and generous, hoping an unbridled self-lessness that made his drawbacks seem beside the point would draw people close to someone as generally useless as himself.

Dennis didn't get out much due to this impairment I'm imagining. But people in his neighborhood would ring his bell whenever they felt sad or problematic. He would listen attentively, so I guess he wasn't deaf, and he would say kind, supportive, wise sounding things in response, which seemed to help them. He wasn't a happy person, even so, but helping people made him feel like he was more than some disabled guy who needed others' prompts to even live and who evinced no value to the world apart from making able people count their lucky stars.

Sometimes these visitors would pause their fretting long enough ask how Dennis was, and he would tell them he was fine as briefly as he could because he knew they didn't really care, or that they wanted to be quickly reassured he was okay enough to always be cemented where they could rely on him, so, in a way, their show of interest was a secret way of making sure he wasn't doing all that well, because they actually wished the worst for him, or wished the worst that wouldn't kill him.

Despite his reassurances, he was very lonely, to tell the truth, meaning when he was alone, which was most of the time. After someone he'd just helped had closed the door behind them, he would stay planted in the chair or on the bed where he'd been listening, feeling emptied out and disappointed and . . . not unloved exactly, because he figured people loved his kindness, or, rather, relied on his kindness, which isn't quite love.

No one imagined what he did when they weren't with him—for instance, that he'd sit or lie around for hours trying to believe that someone he'd helped might love him and not just need his immoderate attention, not caring from where it came or who'd provided it. Everyone assumed, superficially but logically, that someone so selfless wasn't interested in being loved. Actually, the idea of love never even came up when they thought about him. They just thought, "He's so nice."

One of these confessors was a woman, younger than Dennis. She was beautiful, or he thought so, so I guess he wasn't blind. She also seemed to need his kindness more than the others. She visited a lot. When she would ask how he was doing, the questions seemed sincere, although he knew that the intensity of his attraction to her beauty might have made the questions seem sincere when they were simply more polite or guilt-inspired.

He fell in love with her. It was so stupid. He was agonized and embarrassed by this love since he knew he was unworthy, but he tried to let himself believe she visited so often because she cared or even loved him or, at the very least, had missed him. He knew this theory made no sense, and that their closeness was a technicality, and that she'd never fall in love with someone whose body sucked, but he wanted her to love him so badly, and he understood that love, at least in theories proffered by the church, etc., was supposed to be extremely flexible.

Sometimes he thought, She wouldn't let me be so kind and giving and devoted if she didn't love me. He thought, She has to know I wouldn't be so giving and devoted to her unless I was in love. He thought, She wouldn't let me be so obviously in love with her unless she was in love with me in some way. He thought, If she didn't love me, she would tell me to stop doing all these things for her because the fact that she gives nothing but her presence in return would make her feel uncomfortable.

He loved her so incredibly much. When she needed something, no matter how peripherally or trivial, he would spend days on the phone or negotiating streets and local stores with great difficulty, trying to find someone to help him give her what she needed. When she needed money, he lied to her and said he had a lot of money and went deeply into debt so he could give her everything that anyone could ever give another person.

He began to almost think her gratitude was love because, by then, he'd made himself virtually nothing but a source of generosity that just happened to look unpleasant like him. He knew the only way to let her know he loved her was to give and give, ideally greater things than anybody else could give her, and he accepted that the only way he could be loved by her was through being thanked, ideally more warmly than she thanked anybody else.

Something got fucked up later in the movie. I don't remember what it was. Maybe she came by one day and said that something he'd helped her with had made it possible for her to move away somewhere where she'd be happier. That sounds right. In any case, he realized she'd only ever wanted him to help her, period, and now that she was happy, she didn't need him anymore, and that she'd never actually loved him. She'd only loved how much he loved her, if even that. Or she'd only loved that love's results. Or not even loved. Felt lucky.

Dennis recognized that, given what he had to work with, he had, through her inveigling, become the best human being his materials could ever possibly allow to be fashioned from him, the most valuable, the least pointless, and that, even in that utmost state, even after having given her what she or anyone most wanted in the world, happiness, and after devoting everything he had materially and otherwise to her and trashing his emotions to accomplish that, he wasn't loved.

He didn't think, Maybe if I write a novel that would tell her how I feel in a more exalted form, and if it's great enough . . . He wasn't a writer. He hadn't written novels that people liked and whose talent in that one regard formed his only premium in the world. He couldn't think, If I devote this last, most valuable thing about myself to her, and if I tear apart the rules that hold the novel back and write the most amazing ever, it will be such a brazen act of love that she'll have to love me. Unlike me, he had no foolish hopes about himself and art's value and love.

After a few minutes of debate, Dennis killed himself. I can't remember how. Maybe Dennis shot himself in the head, but I would think that. If I didn't remember exactly how it happened, that's obviously what I would guess. There was some kind of funeral. The people he had helped showed up, including the woman. They seemed sad, but not so sad that you thought his death would make much of a difference in their lives. He'd been really nice, and that was nice, but he was disabled, so the suicide made sense.

I've tried to write my version of this depressing novel several times. Or I would have thought of trying to. Sometimes I couldn't find a form magnificent enough to actualize it. Always I knew or felt that to work as hard and painfully as I would need to do to write this self-excoriating thing, I would have to be like Dennis in the movie and write it as a sacrificial gift to someone whom I loved so much that I would do this hardest thing I could ever do as an act of love for him.

For most of his life, Dennis believed the person he had loved the most and would always love above all others was George Miles, a friend for whom he wrote a cycle of five novels in the roughly 1990s. They met when George was 12 and he was 15. George was the strangest, sweetest, and most beautiful boy Dennis had ever seen on earth, and, to his complete amazement, George loved him instantaneously and fiercely. Or he exhibited every sign Dennis recognized from books and daydreams as love.

But when George turned 14, the passion and excitement Dennis roused from him was diagnosed and named by doctors not as love but a form of mania. George was, they said, severely bipolar, and it's true that something scary had begun to warp his love for Dennis. It either came in outbursts, days-long fits of almost violent affection and flirtation, or was cut off by indifferent stares that showed no sign for sometimes weeks.

Still, they thought it was love. They called it that. They fought through every frenzied day and numbing day to prove that theirs was just a heavily embattled love. George's family and friends and doctors and psychiatrists did everything they could to make him understand that Dennis was a trigger, a drug, an idée fixe. Sometimes they'd convince him that excising Dennis was the key and he would look the other way at school until the loneliness felt even worse.

Dennis's friends back then tried everything to make him understand he was obsessed with saving George, and that he couldn't. That the imagination, meaning love, was too loosey-goosey to compete with science or biology, the smartest said. But Dennis stuck, and, years later, not so very long before George shot himself, they finally drew their heaviest weaponry against his illness and started fucking, and they fucked and fucked until George's last and worst depression took over.

Last year, Dennis thought he was equipped to write his *Heart Is a Lonely Hunter*, of course for George. He sat down at his laptop and, for seven months, wrote down everything he remembered from their friendship, beginning with the night they'd met until the day in 1997 when he found out George had killed himself ten years before without his knowing. Dennis recounted everything they'd done and said as honestly and artlessly as he could write, hoping that his pain and lack of styl-ishness would read as hugely more than them.

Even though the effort made him cry more violently and constantly than he'd ever done, and even though it made him think irrationally, throw his head back and yell at nonexistent George, not unlike how the actor in that Rimbaud biopic yells so stupidly at God while scrawling Rimbaud's poems, what he wrote was just cathartic crap, and when he read it over afterward, all he discovered was that everyone but George and him were right about them.

Maybe George loved how fiercely Dennis thought he was amazing and not just too fucked up. When he became officially bipolar, and Dennis started fighting to unearth the gist of that amazing little kid he'd met, George wanted to believe that kid was trapped some-where inside him, and he fought too, and he called the struggle love because Dennis did. But if George didn't love Dennis, and there's no evidence he did, then I guess I never loved him. I loved something else that this is torn from.

XMAS (1970)

Santa Claus does nearly anything he wants because his whole existence is a falsehood. He's completely nice because benevolence is built into his character, and he's also screwed since altruists are self-destructive. He manifests every act of niceness that could be given to a character in fiction, but the acts seem passionless and automatic to our minds because whoever built him either forgot to give him motivation or else thought his premise would only seem realistic if it functioned out of nowhere.

For all the magnanimity, his powers are de facto and burdensome in private. For instance, no amount of selflessness could melt the endless snow and ice that boxes in his outpost of a life into a navigable path, much less a "worth it once you get there" Mount Everest–y kind of thing. That power would be implausible. His kindness makes him lonelier and less real, if anything. He knows a billion people telepathically, but they don't realize he's overhearing them. He's like a hidden microphone. They think everything he does for them is disembodied magic.

He's just the circumstance that causes everyone to get some things they love once annually. They don't care about him whatsoever or wonder what he's feeling when they look at illustrations of him. His fault entirely. He's so nice and nothing else in concept that every portraitist for generations has rendered him with such a shine he automatically deflects thought, and no one even tries to undermine the pleasure he portends with an analysis.

To nearly everyone, Santa Claus is a self-sustaining bore of vast utility, a kind of machine padded and disguised with human attributes that gives out treats as blindingly and without meaning as the sun. He's like the sun dressed up for Halloween: more fattening than fat, unconscionably jolly, with stop sign–colored clothing and no sexual inference whatsoever. No one cares if he's as happy as his features look, or if he's sick or mentally ill just so long as he's dependable. He's not even a he. He's an it.

People think Santa Claus is so abstractly nice he doesn't differentiate between the targets of his kindness. They think he just skims their billions of requests and answers by necessity. They think he's not just moral but inhumanly objective and that, to him, they're traditionally good or bad and, thus, deserve to be rewarded every year or not. They think he thinks in the most average suppositions. They think his brain is almost a computer and his heart is like a Christian church. Actually, they don't even think that. They just think about gifts or no gifts.

This is a secret, but Santa Claus does in fact evaluate his audience and pick out favorites. Whoever made him left that loophole. His mind grows hopelessly enamored with the twists of certain minds he reads on rare occasions, just as we real humans fall for dreamy bodies that have someone else coincidentally inside them. Given his unbelievability and laughable appearance, he knows he'll never warrant love for real, so he tries to pinpoint people whose reaction to his charity is so unsolvable that, upon responding, he thinks the equivalent of "huh."

Since Santa Claus is a kind of genius, he needs to love someone who's very complicated. Yeah, his generosity is actually love. That's not a typo or a slip. It's love without the bombast of eroticism, or at least without the oomph that makes having sex love's ultimatum. Sometimes he thinks that means his love is true and pure, and sometimes he masturbates like anybody else. His emotional deficiency is a big, tragic secret that would be obvious if people loved where gifts come from. Or if they didn't think politely asking is a form of caring.

If Santa Claus can do almost anything, why won't he? Why doesn't he fly his sleigh into the real world all the time? Why won't he give his favorites the gift of liking nice old men and then schmooze them to befriend him? Why won't he use his superpower to manipulate his favorites into loving Santa Claus and make them want to move into the middle of the freezing, bleak nowhere to live with him? Because that wouldn't be kind. His kindness seems so absolute to those who benefit from it, but it's a saintly ruse wherein he hides his loneliness. No one ever thinks to look for pain there.

One day, to stave off a depression, Santa Claus decides he's an artist. He knows enough about contemporary art through handling wealthy folks' requests to guess that fabricating people's wishes into objects and then manipulating people who are in the wishers' inner circle to fork the objects over and take credit for his kindness is sufficiently subtextual to qualify. He knows enough about humanity to understand that, for artists, making things that sell for millions is a decent substitute for being personally loved. He would really, really like to feel like that.

Art upgrades Santa's self-defeating kindness into an associative conceit and makes him feel even more connected to his favorite human, who is, like him, an artist by default. George is the favorite's name. He's 14 now, but Santa's liked him since he asked to have the moon fitted with giant Mickey Mouse ears as his gift for Xmas 1965. George began to call himself an artist when he reached the age when other people wanted more than others' names and looks as an ID because the only other option was a depressive kid who plays guitar ineptly and is a massive drag to be around.

George counts as Artist by Santa's self-serving

definition because the things he wants are physical impossibilities, and his wishes are too misappropriated to qualify as anything but art that's . . . what's that term . . . conceptual. I.e., things that are the things they offer technically but, when recontextualized into a space that's meaningless without them, become ingredients in viewers' newly activated thoughts or, in George's case, that make him not depressed. A pill that cures cancer would qualify, for instance. But even if they're art, George's hopes are like the chimneys through which Santa Claus supposedly can but doesn't scrunch.

So George the artist never follows through. Or, rather, he fashions art's equivalent with every thought he has, but the things that art traditionally inhabits are just too solid to be piggybacked. His ideas remain construction sites, either eking out on a guitar that he can barely play or over-embroiling in his mind. Those who think artists must deliver stuff to qualify assume he's just a wannabe who stares a lot. Or, and this is key, if they're like Santa Claus and feel ambivalent about the object's vaunted status, George is like the concept of, oh, Michelangelo without the disappointing, dated things he actually made.

Sussing George's fantasies for reciprocating

doodads with a checklist in his mitt is the most invig-
orating thing that Santa Claus has ever felt. George
wants items from the real world that challenge even
Santa's knack for manufacturing. Or, rather, things for
which even Santa, the Zeus of gifts, can only supply
the faulty parts. It forces him to think about his talent
literally. George wants things wherein the things'
assembling, which is Santa's forte, is more like hand-
ing things-to-be a menu. For instance, George wants
a gun, or rather his imagination wants to put a gun at
the disposal of his hands, which would consequently
do his far-fetched bidding.

In other words, George wants a gun that would
manifest his way of using it. It could be cocked and
raised and pointed at his head, all within the lexicon
of real guns' functions, but his mind would cause his
hand to make the gun's blast as benevolent as he alone
believes it would be. What George needs from Santa
Claus or anyone isn't just a gun but for the world to
watch and think, Okay, that's scary on the surface, but,
more important, I wonder what he'll want when he
employs it, not that I want to be there and find out.
Huh.

To give George the gun he wants, Santa Claus
would need to turn the world into his illustration à la

everything about *Pinocchio* that makes a piece of wood become a boy and causes children in the real world to think a toy is secretly a universe for the book's duration. It's a brilliant proposition, but since Santa's affability is all-inclusive, he can't just turn mankind into a foil, but he wants to. George is asking, in effect, to have his body formed into a kind of introverted or inverted Santa Claus, but one whose altruism is entirely focused on himself rather than on a billion people.

George is Santa Claus without the willingness to compromise and the reliance on the power of suggestion and the longing for secondhand appreciation from an audience. Still, Santa would excitedly turn gift hounds around the globe into a rapt, amoral crowd scene, and even render them in CGI, fuck them, and even give himself a little gift—love, George's—but George only loves things that look like things that are unrealizable, and Santa has the stupid, overly articulated image problem. He's useful, but he's not George's type.

Santa's tortured. What the fuck is he to do? When Xmas comes, he reluctantly surrenders to the strictures of his practice and searches George's friends and family for someone who has awesome gift ideas that he or she would pass out with sufficient thoughtfulness to land near George's bull's-eye. Someone who could lend Santa's silly workshop's lame-o gifts' effect an undue amazingness. Someone who won't handicap their impact by using them as a currency to buy something untoward from George, for instance sex. And he weirdly finds someone.

Dennis, 17 on this occasion, is someone whom Santa Claus has always vaguely noted, and always thought to help, but nah because what Dennis used to want fell within the realms where Santa has no business or finesse: talent, sex with teenaged pop stars, the ability to kill someone without that person really dying, etc. He was like George, but in a very dark, off-putting way to Santa. Eventually, Dennis became a writer by default, and Santa thought, Okay, here's hoping fiction helps him, 'cos I can't. But something's changed.

Dennis has fallen unobtrusively in love at last, with George and thanks to George. His love seems just the kind of crazy, dead set, blinded type that George could theoretically incorporate. Dennis loves George almost too much for one source of love to bear. Even reading his thoughts is, like, ick. And, like George's art, this love is too onerous and unrealistic to be fully manifested in the love poems he incompetently pens for George, much less register in George's head, which is busy elsewhere spinning damning evidence against himself.

But George susses love from Dennis's persistence, and even feels a bit, remotely, just as Dennis thinks he's being loved when George lets him stick around. To Santa's limited perspective, granted, Dennis is the only person still in George's life who's nuts enough to similarly think, what's stuck behind his staring eyes and bundled in his monosyllabism will, if George can just not kill himself beforehand, eventually define him as a kind of cross between the Andy Warhol of his age group and a budding Jesus but without that myth's control freak–dom and "I know best" didactic shit.

Dennis finally wants something that Santa doesn't have to rack his brains to match. A book. A book that, granted, has more powers of persuasion than any normal looking book, even in the self-help field, and whose linguistic goals are as overzealous as the items on the wish lists made by kids still too mushy brained to realize Santa's not unlike the guy who fixes Mommy's car, and that Dennis doesn't have sufficient talent yet to write and never will, but nonetheless a book. Maybe lots of them. Things. Things that could ostensibly be wrapped and treed.

Still, given that fatal lack-of-talent problem and related hassles, Santa arranges, as a mental exercise, for Dennis to give George the only thing he wants that Santa Claus can easily arrange: a gun. Then he shuts his eyes and fast-forwards through the wrapping and delivery and George tearing off the wrapping, then hits play. George barely smiles, but still. Dennis aka the friend-shaped substitute for Santa feels loved. George puts the barrel in his mouth and pulls the trigger. Blood splatters everywhere. Santa Claus watches this and thinks, I couldn't handle that.

He writes George a make-believe email, meaning George thinks idly about the myth of Santa Claus, edits out the corny parts, and imagines what Santa would say to him if they could correspond. In any case, the email says, Dear George, I understand you like my work, and it would be difficult to explain why much less put my evaluation into words, but I love yours. I love that, just like me, your art flies over people's heads, ha ha. I say that as a fellow victim of the despotism of consensus. I'd really like to know you, face to face, but being made-up leaves me stuck in a supposed mulch. So, here's what I'm going to do.

You have a friend named Dennis, as you know. As I am just a bunch of bullshit, I'm internally revised by every person who has heard about me and imagines what I'd be if he or she were seers. In the huge majority of cases, I'm as simple as that human bauble in the bedtime stories that first brought me to your world's attention—a trite conceit with an absurd appearance, who, if I actually existed, would freak everybody out. I am thereby left alone to do the nonsense liars told kids I can do, and who cares why or how just so long as people get a piece.

The difference in your friend's case is he believes that, if I did exist for real, I could and would give you everything you ever wanted and let him be the guy who hands it out. And he's right, I would do that. I would because I'm nice and you're deserving, and because his love for you is ultra-sympathetic. I can't love, other than in a generalizing way. The whole "Christian love" crap, essentially. I know that's convoluted, but try this. If I were writing this email to Dennis instead, meaning if it were he who was pretending I could write to him, this is what he'd have me say.

Dear Dennis, I'm in 100% agreement with you that George is the most amazing sentient being who has ever lived, and I should know, since I've known everyone, and I've been able to assess them without you humans' thing for physical appearance, so without the lust that that makes a certain segment of you fellows, say, priests and social workers, creepy. I would be happy, no, exuberant to honor your request and give him everything he wants and let you be the stuff's deliverer.

However, I can't tell you if he loves you or make him love you, which I know you didn't ask from me in so many words, but I'm a mind reader. I can't because my specialty is giving things to intermediaries who then autograph and dole them out as if they were their beings' souvenirs. And, to be honest, if George loves you, he doesn't think about it, as far as I can tell. Still, I will suggest, by my admittedly skewed logic, that he must love your generosity at least. Or if that thing + gratitude for thing = love for thing's originator isn't logical, I'm fucked. Giving gifts is all I've got.

Now I'll write to both of you at once, which I'm already doing, actually. I have an idea. It's very simple. We all agree that George deserves as much happiness as anyone on earth could ever feel without physically shattering or something. Well, George doesn't think he "deserves" that per se, he's just desperate that it be made available to him. Some of what would make him happy is too unrealistic even for the likes of beatific me. Or let's say the delivery is punishing. Reality's a line where unrealistic things dissipate into sci-fi or become explosives, and I'm that boundary's bitch.

Still, I'm Santa Claus, right? I exist in a fairy tale, to your minds. I think you guys would really like it here and thrive. Nothing here is circumscribed. At the same time, everything is very simple, right or wrong, and Dennis wants answers. Granted, my life was set in stone, apart from minor contemporizing tweaks each decade, by whoever made me centuries ago, and there are flaws in me, such as how my powers only switch on in the realm of things that can be bought in stores, but, theoretically, I could have been anything, even God in your outlandish concept.

To you, the fairy tale's a cheesy medium that builds physically unsound worlds that one eventually out-grows, and to me a fairy tale is city planning. So, here's what I'm going to do. I think that since the fairy tale becomes a thing that's available in books when it crosses over into your abodes, that makes it some-thing I can give Dennis to give to you. Also, fairy tales aren't Proust or even Stephen King, so, Dennis, you could write one, if, that is, you can lift your pen out of the pornographic slaughterhouse that you call prose for long enough. So you get ready to do that.

The only trick or problem is I think I'll need to be there too. Maybe manifest myself in something that reminds you I'm your fun's provider, even just a logo. There was obviously some reason why you humans felt the need to mediate windfalls of generosity by putting harmless Santa in the middle, and, given Dennis's involvement, no offense, I fear if I'm not co-Svengali, he'll launch a scary avalanche of something. Plus, okay, I'd like to watch, inconspicuously, mind you, even through peepholes masquerading as some unobtrusive bunny, but I have so much else to do here. Let me think.

THE CRATER

Roden was an old volcanic crater situated in an arid patch of Arizona that had been tagged "the Painted Desert" by early settlers of the area. Although the region's coloration was perplexing, humans are impatient with the unknown, and they're quick to dash all mysteries with names. They would rather say, for instance, "Why, that land looks painted" than be excitedly confused by it.

Take this tale itself, in which the crater I just named will be required to think like you and I and converse with similarly thinking, talking animals, and where, even in such odd and irrational surroundings wherein magic is afoot, I will make the characters want their feelings for one another to be clearly identified, or rather one of them.

Roden had been unearthed or carved or born 400,000 years ago by an eruption. It had looked its best when nothing was alive with the IQ to appreciate it other than as something to be scaled or walked around. Eventually the aging cone became its source's barren reminiscence until an artist named James Turrell, who was famous for creating and revising structures that arrested and apprehended light for our perception, spotted it and thought, I love and disrespect this old thing so much that I'll devote my life to molding it into my greatest artwork. And so he started barbering and adding basements and decorating it with skylights. As the years passed, the cone became his imagination's vehicle, or like the member of a cult that looked the same from far away but had been filched of its originality or will.

One day, a prairie dog that had often used the crater's hemmed in cauldron as a place to trap airheaded rabbits, thought to say what everything that lived or grew around it had been too polite to mention.

"I feel like I don't know you anymore," said the prairie dog. "There are all these tunnels and rooms and sculpted bits inside you now, and fences everywhere, and everything is locked so I can't go inside them. It's kind of creepy."

"It's not that I don't miss the days when I just let you have the run of my exterior, but I was just a wound," the crater said. "I suppose I still am, and I suppose I'm only someone's puppet now, and yet I'm still inside here thinking potshot thoughts about the weather, but it's true that I'm diminishing, and soon I'll be a veil."

"You've lost me," said the confused prairie dog.

"Maybe I'm in love with him," the crater said. "Sorry, by him I mean the artist who's curtailed me. You might have seen him. White hair, older guy. He believes in me. I'm not a corpse to him, I'm like a baby. And it really feels like I'm erupting again, just intellectually rather than in goo, and in very slow motion. I think that means the artist loves me too, but I'm never sure if I'm a circumstance that lets him love himself, or if my dirt is as utilitarian as traditional artists' paint. What do you think?"

"No clue," said the prairie dog. "For me, for every

animal I know, you were always a convenience. So, you probably still are. Sometimes humans kill creatures like me, then stuff the corpses and put the dingy shells in a museum. That happened to a friend of mine. Sometimes I wonder if that was good or bad for him. I wonder if humans really know what they're doing. I'm too quote-unquote primitive to know, but they sure do think they know."

"I never used to worry," the crater said. "But now that I'm the matter of an artist's work, I do all the time. I worry I'm a frame. I worry I'm a decoration. I worry why I worry about that. I worry if I'm loved. In many ways, I look forward to being finished off into a cool, silent shape."

That is what the crater said. Indeed, it said much more, but that is the important part.

And the days came, and the days went, and yesterday was the last day. The final stones were laid into the art-work's paths and tunnels, and the grubby chambers were swept blank, and people whom the crater didn't know from Adam started walking through its body and look-ing at the sky through holes chiseled in its epidermis. And it was like when humans' arteries get clogged and they have a massive stroke. The crater was paralyzed. Whatever had been alive inside the crater remained, but it was like the makings of a person in a coma, and what had been gained or lost through the interjections of the artist has nothing to do with this story.

It was in the late fall, and a Thursday, as it happens, when the intern standing guard at Roden's entrance turned his head and thought he saw a figurative cloud or anthropoidal ball of dust materialize upon the crater's rim.

Gradually, a uniquely outlined human colored in and shaped the haze, which wasn't immaterial by then. Or such was the disparity of the coalescing figure that it appeared to have been magically exuded, even though the tale's internal logic led everyone in eyesight to conclude the being's spooky emergence was a matter of some clingy dust puff blowing from the parking lot where it had parked its car like every other visitor.

George is the name "it" was known by in the world from which he'd either driven or been plucked, and that name was kept in place here because, for all his new-found freedom, he wasn't so different.

He was in his early teens, brown hair, shoulder-length, with blue eyes so visibly unused to his surroundings they looked compulsory to observe, like lakes that you've been told are bottomless. He seemed delighted by the crater, madly pushing windblown strands of hair out of his way to get a look, which was good because it and everything inside this tale were gifts to him from Dennis, whose love for George was so far-fetched that he'd decided it would take a fairy tale's preposterous surroundings and their blessing of suspended logic to convince a reader who doesn't want to feel that much for anyone that his love for George was realistic.

Dennis is only relevant within this story in the sense that, at this very moment, he is sitting at his laptop in an apartment in the 8th arrondissement of Paris writing it. Which is to say the less fantastic world beyond this file or paper matters not at all beyond his thoughts' impingement.

George might have been homogenized into the fairy tale's prevailing cuteness if not for his unusual red backpack. It wasn't just an ill-advised aspect of his outfit, it seemed horribly alive, less belted to his shoulders than riding roughshod. At times, it looked as empty and deflated as a corpse's ventilator, and, at others, stormy like a bag in which some monkey was imprisoned, and, at still others, tightened and balloon-esque or like what you'd get if someone trash-compacted Santa Claus.

To the guard taking George's ticket at the entrance, and to others of Roden's employment who, as by-products of this fairy tale, thought nothing about weirdness, the red backpack was far less telling than it is to you. It was only notable to them in that it seemed to hold a secret, or was perhaps the squirming fetus of a separate, even mistakenly included character that Dennis had neglected to entirely finish. Truth be told, it was this story's beating heart.

For the next few hours, George traversed the crater's underground observatory. In the vestibules that formed the tunnels' intersections, he stood or sat, staring up and through the apertures that monopolized each ceiling. As he watched, the views markedly transformed from simple sky chunks into optical illusions in which the sky was the ingredient, and finally into agencies that got George high on nothing but his eyesight. He felt that he was seeing light as he previously knew it but had never seen, even when his eyes were stoned. He was his eyes' investigator, and they, internally enriched, grew beautiful, distracting every passerby who noticed him. There were even whispers that his eyes must be a facet of the artwork, perhaps hired performers. One particularly enchanted woman wondered to a friend if the young stranger's eyes might even be transplanted nuggets of the light itself onto which his irises and pupils had been painted like the crosshairs on a target.

It was in the final vestibule that George felt the

outsized presence of an older, very bearded man, who, like himself, was lingering much longer than the other tourists. He appeared to be more interested in George than in the artwork. Either that or he seemed to need to view the light's fanfare by a more roundabout procedure, maybe like how viewers of solar eclipses must use mirrors or destroy their eyesight.

Even in the room's vague light, George thought he recognized the man from photos he had seen of James Turrell, the crater's artist, but he was fully cognizant that he was in a fairy tale wherein masks were indistinguishable from faces, so he tried to see him as a cryptic point of interest, knowing only that, since Dennis was controlling everything, whoever the obsessed guy was, George was not in any danger.

Eventually, George found himself outside again, sitting on the crater's rim, very close in fact to where he had originally appeared. Near him, but not suspiciously so, sat the unusually interested and bearded man, engrossed in watching George's face absorb the crater he was undividedly looking into and across.

"You're James Turrell," George said finally. "Or Santa Claus in a very light disguise. One or the other, aren't you? Or both? I guess that's also possible."

"I'm actually Dennis," said the man, "as is everything,

excepting you. But, yes, I'm James Turrell as well. Dennis has mocked up my appearance, and you could say my mind is mine, but my voice is subject to his razor. If you'd like to think of me the way he wants, and forgive me for the self-absorbed comparison, I'm who I am, and he's something like the frame through which my light is pouring. So I'm him, but I don't consist of anything that isn't me, is what I mean." At that, he smiled sheepishly. "It seems I'm not an easy man to replicate. And what's in that?" He pointed at the odd red backpack, which was wiggling a little.

"I don't know," George said. "I just think it needs to be here. Some kind of portal or a plug." At that, he gave the man an almost plaintive squint. "Honestly, I hope it's a gun. But I think it might be Santa Claus. That's a long, depressing story—my 'wishing it's a gun' thing— and I know I sound ridiculous in any case."

"If I weren't mostly an infection, I would prob-ably agree with you," said James Turrell, who nodded sagely. "So, what did you think of my work?" he added, nodding toward the entrance, or, rather, toward the sign that read ENTRANCE with an arrow underneath because the opening itself was microscopic from that distance.

"Oh, amazing, fun, very fun, trippy, mind-altering,

I love it," George said enthusiastically, but when he looked at James Turrell, the artist seemed unsatisfied. "Words aren't my talent," he continued. "I'm more of a soundproof kind of person. So those words I used were leaks. But what happened in me when you asked was quite intense."

"This might be strange to say, or, perhaps, to hear," said James Turrell, "but the reason I've been watching you so closely is not entirely for your beauty, although there is that, or that bonus. That's to say, as I've scrutinized your eyes, I've felt as though I'm viewing my manipulations of the light from your perspective, and . . . wow. Given the impracticality of touring the world with you along as art, and given that we're in a fairy tale, and that, off in the real world where we'll live again one day, my crater has remained untouched, flaws and all, I'm drawn instead to the idea of allowing you to mess around with it, add your two cents, perfect it, or the opposite. Carte blanche. Simple as that. I'm not flirting with you, honestly, I'm not."

George thought about the offer for a while, weighing how completely he'd been blown away and, if not or only semi-, when. "Okay," he said finally. "Do you have any earthmoving equipment?"

Not long thereafter, George was seated in the cab of

a yellow mini-excavator that was parked and rumbling on a ridge that overlooked the crater.

Since Dennis has quick-cut this fairy tale to here, it's unclear if the excavator had been parked somewhere nearby and moved there as a gift from James Turrell, or whether it had been magically excreted by the baffling red backpack, which had suddenly revealed one of its métiers while things were paused.

For a while, James Turrell stood by the open door, watching George decide, or, to be more accurate, stare, pointedly or accidentally, through the windshield, maybe in the throes of some aesthetic formulation, or maybe wishing he had asked the artist for a gun instead and was about to kill himself, or already had, since George quite often thought he was the problem with everything.

Between George's lengthy quiet time and the bodily dilapidation that cribbed people in their early 70s, James Turrell eventually felt defeated by himself and sat down on a nearby rock to watch things more dispassionately.

After an hour or maybe slightly more, George bounced back. He leaned close to the windshield, studying the rocky ground before him. Using the excavator's dashboard knobs and levers, he dropped its bucket to the earth. Then, edging the serrated lip ever closer to the rim, he gradually pushed and scraped a thin covering of topsoil until it finally reached the edge and spilled into the crater's maw, then raised the boom and checked to see if anything seemed different.

As he watched, the excavator's cab began to rock and sway, as it might have in an earthquake that was violent enough to wobble such a heavy vehicle. More inexplicably, from deep within the long, dead cauldron, a noise began to issue. To George's ears, it sounded not unlike a human yawn, but much louder than what a simple mouth could generate. Even the excavator's churning mechanisms could not stifle it.

A sharp but not unpleasant fear of the unknown enveloped George, and he looked to where he'd last seen James Turrell. Turrell was sitting on a rock, still watching George. He seemed completely unperturbed by the booming tone, or even deaf to it, or even of the mind that George's efforts had created it, so much so in any case that, upon seeing George acknowledge him, he gave an earnest thumbs-up.

Everywhere George looked, the cacti and brush were not so much as trembling, and the tourists he could see off in the distance walked as steadily as ever. He could only then conclude that the weird event was happening in his head.

By now the yawn had disarranged itself into what sounded very like the kinds of stretched-out, muddled words pronounced by someone waking up. Although the crater's rim was not revised, or not enough to bring a massive set of lips to mind, it seemed evident to George that the crater was the noise's author, and that it was communicating, or attempting to, or being spoken through by something human, and was being incorrectly used, if so, the way throat singers do their necks.

"Can I ask you something?" the voice gradually managed to enunciate. "That is, if you can understand me. I have a feeling that you do, although I've never previously known a human that could hear me. Even James Turrell, my mentor, always swats the air around his ears when I say hi. Mine is a very alienated life, but I am used to it."

George thought and thought some more. "Sure," he said at last, "if I can do the same. Talking to an artwork of your quality is pretty huge for me."

"Then why," the voice asked. "Why did you do that? Why change things? And before you think my words impertinent, if you do, know I've asked James Turrell this question on hundreds of occasions, and, at times when he was touring and I was being doctored by the men he'd hired, I asked them. At first the question was a real one, but having been ignored by everything but my imagination, I first learned I have one, and once I had acknowledged it, it began to answer me, or I began to answer. It's nice to ask someone who isn't me and is not a prairie dog or rabbit. They're like babies. So here's the bigger question. When I was being sculpted, I felt loved. But in the months since I've been stilled, or maybe stunned would be more accurate, I haven't felt that, which is strange since I've only been declared the prompt for love considerably more often since I died, that is, if you believe what people walking through my body say, which I feel I should."

George hadn't expected to be addressed so personally, and he felt uncomfortable that all the questions he'd been devising for the crater were as if it were the whole earth's spokesman.

"I'll try to answer you," George said, "but first, and I'm not sure how to ask you this, or if the question is rhetorical, but are you the artwork, or are you just the crater where it's situated?"

The crater thought about that painfully, or so it somehow seemed to George. "I see what you're saying," it said.

"Well, that's good since I don't know what I was saying, or not exactly," George said, smiling.

"When I felt loved by James Turrell," the crater said, "I think it was because of what he reasoned I had been, fiery, ten times taller, and what my carcass could return to being with his specialty's assistance, so what he'd loved was what my premise did to his imagination, and I was just, who knows?"

There came a silence fraught enough that George hazarded a guess. "His friend?" he ventured. "Or, wait, his sort of . . . paraplegic friend?"

"That's interesting," the crater said. "One afternoon not long before I hardened, a wealthy man, extremely old, quite enfeebled, whom James Turrell was courting for donations, arrived by limousine to check the merchandise. He was in a wheelchair, sort of dangling there, but because his idle body had the money needed to complete the chamber in my northwest side, if I remember right, James Turrell pushed the guy's wheelchair for hours, which isn't easy on this coarse terrain, and talked so charmingly to him, even though he couldn't talk himself or maybe even hear, or maybe even think at all, he was that decrepit, and I thought, How am I not a topographical 'that guy'? Necessary but not infinitesimally loved. You want to know about depression? By the way, that man, or, rather, someone employed by him whose brain was functioning, gave James Turrell the money.

Ten million dollars. Hence, everybody's happy. I should be grateful."

"That makes sense," George said quite carefully because, in truth, the crater had begun to bore him. "I used that word love about you too, but if you were to ask me now, 'Do you?' I might say yes, but it would be to calm you down. You see, that question, simple as it probably seems to you, is very stressful when you know the answer that its speaker's hoping for. In your case, yes, I did, but that was when I thought you were just here for me. Now that I know you better and realize that I don't know you in the slightest, and when you're less an art-work I'm so glad I saw than like a massive growling lion face whom I feel I must appease, I'm not sure."

"I don't understand," the crater said. "But consider-ing that I have a mind composed of dirt and rocks, some retardation would be natural. And then there are these inelastic words I'm asked to speak."

George nodded. "Mine too," he said. "I feel like I'm pronouncing them phonetically."

There was a lull as George, the crater, and maybe others, the prairie dog, unpacked what they'd been made to say and privately compared that to their normal output—faint earth rumbles, barks, words but not a lot of them in George's case.

The sparkliness and vaguely psychotropic mien that had given the location a sufficient dash of weirdness to authenticate their dialogues, and which no one had even noticed was unrealistic, dialed back until the setting was your average desert, them thirsty in it. Everything was technically the same, with the possible exception of George's backpack, which had noticeably sagged and looked no redder than a thousand stylish others.

"So what's in the knapsack," the crater asked.

"A gun," George said.

At that, George and the crater reached an impasse, or, rather, my imagination reached an impasse, and I closed my laptop. But the strangest thing happened.

As I had never written fairy tales before, I thought it was the same as writing an experimental novel, and that the characters and stories littering the prose were just like nuts embedded in its fudge, and that to close my laptop's lid would simply store the tale-in-progress, maybe slightly refrigerate it. But this was not the case, or not entirely.

For fairy tales are a form in which the characters and story, for all their falseness, are the sum and substance, and where language merely chisels them to some degree.

So the fairy tale adjusted, and, as my laptop's lid descended, a massive UFO or sheet of metal plunged out of the sky above the crater. Before George or James Turrell or anyone could wonder why the sun had set so promptly and off schedule, it struck the earth and squashed or murdered everyone and everything, even the brawny excavator, like mosquitoes.

THE HEART
IS A LONELY
HUNTER

My school was so private, i.e., more or less 300 students, 5th grade to 12th, all boys, that when it threw us after-hours dances, the janitor and coach would switch the light bulbs in the ceiling of the cafeteria for colored ones and stack the chairs and tables in the corners.

I was 15, which makes it 1968, and at a dance with my brainy stoner friends. Jay was yelling in my ear about his little brother who was freaking out on LSD. He said he was too stoned to deal with that and thought of me because I'd done a lot of LSD but wasn't high right then, unusually.

I would have helped since I was always sort of knee-jerk worried.

The first time I saw George, he was walking on his tiptoes with his arms straight out and waving them around as if his shoes were balanced on a tightrope and the asphalt was mist.

He had long hair like me, and, even though it was too dark to see more than that hair and what he wore, I knew I'd never seen him at our school before, since I would have seen a boy that young with hair that long, and that was probably because the school kept kids away from teenaged students for our mutual protection.

"This is Dennis," Jay said to him and then careened away.

"I've heard of you," the boy said.

"What's happening?" I asked him as I often did instead of saying hi back then.

"My feet are huge," he said. "I can't walk."

"Are you scared?" I asked.

"Of my feet, yes," he said.

I told him I had taken lots of LSD and maybe understood what he was going through, and that some friends of mine had helped me down to earth when I was losing it, and I thought their scheme could work on him if he would let me try, and I guess that's when I put my hand out.

"What's that for?" he asked.

"Take it," I said.

"It's too small," he said.

If he'd had shorter hair, or if the acid hadn't made him seem more me-like than an average kid, I might have done what you're supposed to do with children, say, grabbed his hand against his will since I knew more than him and thought, He'll thank me once he isn't high or young.

"No offense," I said. I slid my arms beneath his, raising him until his legs were waggling an inch or so above the ground, then trudged to where the ground's concrete was cast more solidly and had no texture so to speak and brought no imagery to mind. I set him down and started sliding out my arms.

"No," he said, and clutched my hands before they could escape. "I need them."

"I'm going to do a thing," I said, "and you should let me do the thing, and all you have to do is walk or stumble. Is that cool?"

I would say he laughed, but even as a kid, George

was always very cautious when he laughed like someone sickly coughing in tight, crowded quarters. "You're
trying to talk to me," he said.

I started walking us away. His shoes fishtailed between
mine, but we gradually made it to the school's athletic
field. I steered him toward the baseball field, then
toward its closest base—third, I think—where I low-
ered us. That left him sitting in my lap, which felt too
gay to me, so I tried to slide him off onto the ground.
He fought me and kept saying, "No, please don't," but
between my pushing and his clinging, we wound up in
a compromised position wherein his ass was resting on
the dirt, and he had two fistfuls of my T-shirt, and his
legs were hooked around my waist, and my arm was
clamped across his shoulders.

"Now, tilt your head back and look at the stars," I
said, "and try to think of me as boring."

His eyes checked out the sky. His chin raised, and,
after saying "wow" a few times and scrunching up my
T-shirt's chest into two ugly flowers, his face was over-
ridden by an acidheaded look, as unmistakable as Down
syndrome, wherein one's eyes misfired, completely
lost their windows-of-the-soul effect, and just looked
cretinous to people who were sober.

He stayed weird faced for quite a while, minutes or

longer even. I guess I must have looked around the field, and listened to the psychedelic music leaking from the windows of the cafeteria, and tried to give the stars some benefit of the doubt.

At some point, George turned his eyes on me. From straight on, they looked extremely frightened, but a look of fear was also one of LSD's reliable yet specious decorations. "Am I crazy?" he asked me, or maybe asked somewhere to which he thought I was the doorman.

"No, you're high," I said.

"I don't mean now," he said. "I mean all the time."

"I just met you," I said.

By then his eyes had stalled on mine. I guessed his mind was off investigating some hallucination, and that my eyes were just like buttons on a shirt to him or else seemed very far away and safe like stars. It's always disconcerting when a little kid stares at you, because you could be doing something un-thought-out that will change his life by accident, so I looked away.

"No, come back, I'll fall," he said.

I looked at him again. Not being stoned, I didn't have the expertise to use his eyes as microscopes to help me solve some mystery about the universe in which I formed particle. I remember thinking, They only look like eyes, they're just eyes-like on the surface, and, even if they're eyes, they're too full of camouflage to see me or tell I'm sentient, at least if I don't move much.

So, I was stuck exploring what he actually looked like. First his eyes, which, even given they were sitting ducks, let out nothing personal that I could see or riff imaginatively upon. Other than their blue color and dilated pupils, acid had completely padlocked them. I couldn't see a thing I hadn't seen in mine in mirrors, and even less, and I remember killing time by trying to assess their corneas and glossiness and lenses like an optometrist.

I checked and multiply rechecked his eyebrows, nose, lips, cheekbones, chin, forehead, their placement, and the minutiae of his face's pores for what felt to me like hours, but couldn't have been hours. I must have had so many concepts and hypotheses about his face to keep my eyes fixated there and interested, but all I can remember was deciding he was cute, or maybe just adorable since he was 12.

Now when I concentrate and visualize that face I must have memorized and come to know more thoroughly than any other face that's ever looked at me not from a photograph, what amazes me is that I don't think it confused me or attracted me, and that I couldn't have imagined kissing it or wishing I could script my name with an affectionate inflection into its voice if I'd even wanted to.

Eventually, I saw something crop up in his eyes. A kind of energy that might have formed a plus sign, if it were an image. I guessed it was the starting point of what he thought of me

"Are you back?" I asked.

"You just talked to me," he said.

"I did," I said.

"You won't believe what I just thought," he said. "It wasn't even thought."

"And what was it?" I asked.

He turned his head and looked out at the field. He pried his fingers from my shirt and swung his legs off mine, then crossed them and sat up straight so he could face whatever he was seeing. My arm was still around his shoulders, which felt obnoxious, so I started to remove it until I felt his fingers squeeze and tug my wrist. "No," he said. "I still need that."

I think we sat there looking at the grass and making mental hay while I asked him things like "You okay?" and "How's it going?" now and then.

I heard the music shut off in the cafeteria. Since it had a psychedelic tinge, its loss was more significant to someone stoned than not, and, sure enough, without that sound George seemed to turn off too, or rather turn on, or I mean he either animated and became the slightly nervous seeming little kid I guessed he'd been before he drugged himself and met me, or I saw that. I raised my arm, but instantly his hand reached up and grabbed my forearm in midair and pulled it down again.

"Not yet," he said.

"The dance is over," I said. "How normal are you?"

"I'm . . ." he said then waited for a while. "Half."

I noticed he had stiffened, especially his back and neck, and gripped my arm as if he wanted to say something else and couldn't, but he kept looking at the field while nothing happened, and I decided he was probably as close to being ready as he would be.

"There's something wrong with me," he said finally.

"Like what?" I asked.

"I can't tell," he said and looked directly at me.

His eyes were working, and they were hard to meet, like kids' eyes always are, and I couldn't tell what they were thinking, or if it was about me, and didn't realize I'd ever want to know.

I must have been relieved to know a face was back where it belonged, by which I guess I mean a face I didn't need to take as seriously, or that I didn't think I could relate to anymore, but I remember feeling disappointed that he was just a kid, or still a kid, and how that feeling frightened me.

"I looked at you for a really long time," he said, "but I still don't know you."

I WISHED

When I was 10 years old, some friends and I were playing in some bushes on an edge of my front yard that very roughly brought to mind a pint-sized forest. One of them was using an old rusted ax to chop depressions in the ground for some forgotten reason, and I was crawling wildly through the shrubbery below, I don't know why. My friend chopped. The ax blade split my skull. If he hadn't semi-seen me and let up slightly on the handle, I would be dead.

I was squashed onto the ground, out cold and with a volcanic vent-like wound erupting in my budding hippie hair. My friends freaked out and ran away, leaving me to die or live somehow or other. When I woke back up at some convenient point, my head was firing blood in all directions so I struggled to my feet and ran screaming up the driveway.

I was salvaged, then kept out of school for months, recovering in bed. For the first few weeks, the pain was unbelievable. They couldn't anesthetize my head because my brain was trapped inside so there was nothing anyone could do. I kept wishing I was dead. I turned my thoughts into a beacon that sent a nonstop SOS, or the opposite, I guess, to God or whoever, and I absolutely meant it, but I also knew it wouldn't happen.

When the pain eventually waned a bit, and I could think of things I would be doing were I not in bed or incapable of moving even an inch without a pounding headache, it began to interest me that I had wanted to die even though I knew I wouldn't, no matter how passionately I'd wished to be dead and how much death was the only thing that could have helped me.

I felt as though my wish for death contained a kind

of logic that I couldn't access with my usual overly protective thoughts. That, prior to then, I'd been a kind of actor or self-hypnotist, not just when I socialized with other people but when I even thought of other people, which, put together, constituted almost always. That my wish had been completely understanding because it knew me, unlike my friends.

I felt that when I'd wished to die, I was being who I really was, sans interference from the world or from the priorities and hopes that had polluted me through other people's minor needs for me or from the books I read incessantly. It was like I'd found myself, and I was someone who had never had the things I really wanted, plainly never would, and whom no one would fully comprehend. I think that saved me more than surgery.

After that, I began to make a wish when the impracticalities of life wronged me, but very cautiously. I did that to understand who I really was and what I actually wanted, regardless of whether my wish could possibly come true or was good or bad for me or for anyone else, because I didn't know who I was most of the time.

I tried to see myself as consciousness that looked like me and whose speaking voice was based herein and censored by my crappy English but also out of my control like my ventriloquist. I used that voice to represent the public me. And then there was my secret self who took pity on how compromised I usually was and poached the wisest powers of my mind, then used a thought to say, in so many words, "I will grant you one wish, Dennis. What do you want?"

Then I would think about the question until it had infected me, revising and refining a related wish, first conceptually as a tryout to assess the consequence, were it to happen in the real world. If the wish involved sex, which it almost inevitably did, I would test myself by masturbating, cum, then reappraise the wish more puritanically and decide if my surpassing goal of cumming had overly influenced me or given me the equivalent of truth serum.

This process might go on and on for weeks, months, with one offhand in-process wish refining and dwindling until I'd built the single most intransigent, comprehensive thing I craved and that would never come to pass and that no one else could ever guess I wanted. And once I had decided on and made that perfect wish, didn't get it, and accepted that my peace of mind was doomed, I thought I knew exactly who I was, and I stopped wishing for it.

I thought my wishing ritual would die away or be co-opted when I became a writer, or at least a writer good enough to do my thoughts some kind of justice and get them published and read. I assumed the writing thing was generated from the same impulse I'd had to pinpoint and set aside my deepest shit. I figured writing would just give that stuff a solid form and, if safely sealed into the envelopes of books, readers could solve me if they wanted. But that wasn't true.

Instead, my writing merely subdivided me again. I became a semi-guy who dealt with other people nicely and another semi-guy who used the written word to challenge readers to accept the secret me selectively and still another semi-me who wanted something so abnormal that even the unrivaled distancing device of nuanced, airtight wordage couldn't get it out to other people.

What the writing did was draw a stylized map to the general location where my wishes were impregnating. I tried to make the maps clever, funny, disturbing, and erotic so the things I wrote about would seem as scary or exciting to envision as they'd been to pen, sort of like the rosy illustrations with which rides are represented in the folded maps they hand you at the entrances of amusement parks.

I think the wishes always courted love. I think somewhere along the line I decided that I hadn't actually wanted to be dead when I'd wished to die, and that I'd wanted death to love me enough to kill and take me. I don't think I knew that for a long time, though. I think I thought the wishes I so time-consumingly constructed were about having raucous sex since that was the crux of what happened in them.

When I never thought I could be loved, or not realistically, or not by anyone real who had a choice, by which I mean people other than my family, which covers most of my life, I'd think up situations where the horror of not being loved, of being rejected by someone I could ostensibly pick out of the lineup of Los Angeles's cutest boys, for instance, would feel the most intense.

And since cumming was the most intense outcome I knew, I made them hugely sexual, and, to try to make the blast as wild as I imagined being loved would feel, I made my fantasies as scary and chaotic to everyone involved in them as possible, but especially to me since I was real. I wanted the orgasms they produced to be like self-inflicted fatal wounds, or maybe more like being shocked back into real life by a defibrillator, I guess.

When I was really young, I wished quite warily, as if a wish was a new car and I its freshly licensed driver. I thought that if I wished to alter people in my real life, I would get too confused about them and myself and go crazy or something. So I would fixate on, say, cute young actors on TV shows or cute young pop singers because they were as blank and unrealistic as the secret me.

I thought those wishes would be safe to play within, and they could vanish from my memory like books of fairy tales from growing children's bookshelves, which they did, apparently, because I don't recall anything about the huge majority of them, apart from one wish that seems to have been so taxing to perfect that I tried to keep its doings straight in a diary that I found among my stuff some years ago.

That wish, which I revised sometimes hourly over several weeks when I was 13, involved identical twin brothers who were actors on a short-lived TV show I liked. *The Monroes* was the show, and it was set in the wilderness of Montana maybe, back when families pioneered out west by wagon train, then squatted plots of forest, built cabins, and tried to start new anarchistic lives of endless promise or whatever.

The twins, played by wan, long-haired, adolescent actors Keith and Kevin Schultz, were the youngest of some siblings whose parents had been killed by Native Americans or something, and who consequently had to organize themselves into a family unit, with the oldest brother-sister combo as the makeshift mom and dad and the twins reformulated as mock sons whom the others had no choice but to control.

They twins were very cute, presumably to get young girls to watch, but they couldn't act at all. To make them function properly, the show's director had them speak in almost monotones, and hold their faces very still, and even move their bodies stiffly. They seemed eternally bored, even when required to come off angry or frightened or hysterical, which made them boring to watch, I would imagine, unless you were attracted to their looks like I was, in which case they were addictively mysterious.

The twins were mostly there to illustrate the vexing obligations of their older siblings. Even so, they seemed more like family cats, free-floating tidbits who came and went a few times in every episode, and whose appearances were noticed by the others more than greeted with affection. My guess is that, had their older siblings shown the wooden duo too much interest, it might have made them seem obsessed like pedophiles.

So the twins were asked to be peripherally in trouble all the time, i.e., to get captured by outlaws, almost eaten by bears, fall in ravines, contract malaria, etc., and thereby advance the story lines at large and display their minor characters' bravery and foolishness without sapping much attention from their older siblings' weekly tested skills as decent parents.

They were like mistakes or weaknesses, and I seem to have decided that a well-appointed wish could be the perfect opportunity to enhance their roles and also figure out my fascination with them, and, by proxy, better come to grips with the unavailability of everyone I craved romantically or sexually but had no guts or looks to help bewitch.

According to my notes, my wish started its short, roiling life respectfully. I wished that I were living in the same fictional Old West component of the TV show, and that the twins weren't bad actors but incredibly laconic historic figures, and that my parents also had been killed by Native Americans or something, whereupon the older siblings reluctantly adopted me.

My premise as the new son was to show Keith and Kevin Schultz the interest no prior cast member was scripted to—gambling that, deep inside, they were dying for attention, and that I could undermine their catatonic bents and get all three of us laid. But I quickly realized my mistake. Their relentless stoicism wasn't rubbery. It had been set in stone by lack of acting talent, and my wish made no allowance for off-show groundwork.

So I couldn't tell if being in cahoots with them and flirting merely added "dealing with the gay son" as a recurrent subplot of their general malaise. They seemed more hypnotized by me than really interested, and, given my neediness and wish to get my boner back to dangling unnoticed in my pants, where it belonged, that got frustrating fast.

So I revised the wish. I became a "bad kid" who'd been cast to use the duo's diffidence to easily convince them that, say, smoking pot, then having sex with me was no more challenging than looking frightened by a man dressed as a bear. Getting naked with their cute but rigid bodies sated me in one sense, but, once I'd cum, I still felt hurt by how they'd just go back to staring blanks at me again.

Next I wished that one of them would fall in love with me, even if he couldn't show it, and that the other twin would get so jealous underneath his placid surface that he'd kill his brother in a violent rage. I found that upgrade interesting, according to my notes, because, given that they looked and thought—or, rather, barely thought—alike, the murder felt less like tragedy than just subtraction or streamlining.

Excited, I spent several days' entries wishing the fratricide was ever more appalling. As this wish predated my acquaintanceship with Sade, it wasn't all that gory. Its violence merely showed me what his stolid face could not, that he felt violently in love. In short, he clobbered his dead ringer's head with rocks while I smiled lovingly with horror at him. Oh, I should say I felt no guilt, because the killer twin had tied me to a chair, forcing me to watch.

But at some point, I realized there was something missing even so. I wanted Keith and Kevin Schultz to know that I was me and not another actor doing something in their scripts that occasioned them to wildly overact. So I further upped the ante and made my wish more God's-eye-like. I turned the sets and premise of the show into the falsities they were, and I made the twins and me young actors who worked therein and lived in Hollywood or someplace.

I made the TV show's director some super-evil guy who was so obsessed with Keith and Kevin Schultz that he'd concocted and bankrolled a fake TV show and "cast" them in it as a way to get them nude and raped and so on. I had him use the show's cabin set like people who make snuff films use the basements where they drag their captives. And I was in the cast too, but tied to a chair again.

But in asking for the Schultzes to be real like me

with lives and friends and shit I'd need to know about to represent them, I hit a wall. The only tip-offs were in magazines like *Tiger Beat*, whose mission was to edit every star they lionized into the perfect chick bait. Just like every other idol, Keith and Kevin were portrayed as nice, reserved young boys whose love for girls was as inclusive as the printed text inside a Valentine.

That limitation might have been no big deal were I a normal masturbating kid, but my wishing thing was much more serious, as I've explained. I saw my wishes as a kind of life or death decision, and I wanted what I wished for to defeat me when it couldn't come to life. And no matter how I overhauled the Schultz twins, they were never worth it. The last sentence of my wish journal was "Fuck them."

In my later teens, I discovered serial killers, as they were termed. I decided they were like primordial big brother figures of my wishing side. The dick without the brains, essentially. Haunting that resource solved my wishing's problem for a while. Because the murdered boys were baffling and safe like TV characters, and almost real, or real enough since they originated in the news, but not dangerously real since, by the time I knew they'd even been alive, they were dead.

Suddenly the sex I wished on real boys seemed

psychologically okay, like throwing lit firecrackers at somebody in a coffin. To read the news reports that summed the victims up as prostitutes or drug addicts or mentally unsound, the promises their lives had made to them and everyone were so slight that you could see why horny psychos could have rationalized their murders as simple edits.

I got particularly obsessed with Robert Piest, who was the last boy killed by John Wayne Gacy, and the crime that eventually led to his arrest. I liked the way Piest looked, which, at least in rugged newsprint, was eerily like George Miles, who, as you know by now, I wanted desperately to love me, but who was too erratic looking to objectify into a cute guy you could have by stripping naked, so I didn't.

So Piest, with his frozen face and untold body language and physique finagled by high school gymnastics, as the news squibs always mentioned, presumably to add zeal to the nightmare he'd been through, became a kind of storage space and match for George, and in my secret world where I had never dared to bring him, he and Piest grew almost indistinguishable.

I liked that Piest was not a drug addict or prostitute or criminal like Gacy's other casualties, and, thus, vaguely less doomed to die young anyway, which gave his death the air of devastation I would need to even start to try to think it could relate tangentially to George's. At the same time, Piest was termed in every thumbnail obit as being, while brighter than Gacy's other gambits, unmotivated. He wanted to grow up to work in a garage, if I remember right.

Gacy had always denied himself boys as relatively valuable and more than likely to be missed than Piest, but there was something to the boy that turned him, maybe even, I imagined, the same who-knows-what that made me target George's love over that of people who could feel and show it. And there was something so momentous about killing Piest, compared with Gacy's others, that what's known about the death is legendary among serial killer buffs for its poetic.

What's known for sure is Gacy spotted Piest somewhere, decided to kill him, and offered him some kind of easy-money short-term fix-up job at Gacy's house, and that Piest accepted and showed up at Gacy's to do said job at some appointed time. After that, no one really knows, but either Piest balked when he discovered the job was getting fucked, or Gacy was so intimidated by Piest's quality he couldn't get a hard-on. So, instead of raping Piest, he said something like, "Let me show you my rope trick, and I'll let you go."

Gacy put some kind of quirky noose thing made from rope tied onto sticks around Piest's neck and turned the sticks, then watched the boy strangle to death. When Piest died, Gacy looked up at a light bulb that was hanging from the ceiling, and something apparently profound happened in Gacy's head that no one will ever know and that even Gacy said was indescribable, and he looked with fascination at the light bulb, and said, "Light."

I wanted to understand what "light" meant and why Gacy hadn't raped Piest when he could have so handily, and I wanted not to be someone so covert and disconnected that I would let someone who could be George get killed. So, I set the time clock in a wish to just before Gacy had snuffed Piest and made myself his hopelessly crushed-out friend who always tagged along with him, and I let Gacy just be Gacy because I'd always had a hard time imagining the impetus of murderers from scratch.

I made dozens if not hundreds of wishes set in a slightly altered version of the real-life crime scene. I was there, trapped but not cute enough to be killed with any excitement or something, so I was cruelly forced to not just watch my hopeless crush get offed but to never even see him naked much less fuck him. That was where my wish was concentrated, trying with my magic powers to reorganize that horrible, depressing situation.

For a while, I tried to turn the murder's buildup into a kind of courtroom scene with Gacy as the judge and me acting as my own attorney, sometimes under the guise of representing Piest's best interests and sometimes using him as evidence against himself that I had brought before the court to serve my own. Since Gacy had the final word, and it was mine, the case seemed very open and shut to me.

For instance, I would say to Gacy: If you kill him, you'll get caught. He'd say, "If I let him go, he'll tell, and I'll get caught anyway." Then why not rape him first, I'd ask. "Because he's too good for me." All the more reason. "Tell that to my dick." Then let me fuck him. "I thought he was your friend." He is, but you're going to kill him, so it's my only chance. Plus, you could watch. "But if it turned me on, I'd kill you too." Then don't watch, just let me fuck him because . . . why not and what's the difference?

When Piest was on the witness stand, I'd say, If I kill Gacy, which I can because this situation is my wish, will you love me? He'd say, "Well, maybe by default." What if I said you're going to kill yourself when you turn 30, and your life will get more hellish, and I'm the only one who'll love you even when you're insufferable. "If it's hellish anyway why bother?" To not be so alone. "I've been alone and suicidal ever since we met." Then if I kill Gacy, let me fuck you. "Why?"

Long story short, I tried every rationale that reality had stuck me with to coerce Gacy into either sparing Piest's life or allowing me to fuck him first, and, in later, more developed versions, I even called a clinician to the witness stand and used what seemed like basic logic to convince him to sell Piest on why loving me was good for him, period, and clever too since maybe, just maybe, even a psychopath like Gacy might respect love's stature and let us leave.

Things got grittier and juicy over time but I'll spare you. No matter how I tweaked the wish, it never brainwashed Piest, someone with every reason in the fucking world to love me, or to lie convincingly at least. And what finally killed it off—and this sounds convenient, but it's true—is I took acid, bought into its mind-trumps-body doctrine, and exposed my wishing's fatal flaw. Sex, or rather lust: Gacy's, Piest's lack thereof, and mostly mine since it began that stupid swordfight.

That took me back to where my wishes started, the hankering to die, and how huge and pure and terrifying and extremely selfish and yet arguably selfless that had been. I realized my ambition had been hacked along the way, and I'd ended up like Orson Welles—I think was my comparison—except I was too horny to create another masterpiece rather than too broke. So I masturbated to the point where having sex seemed like a yawn, then made one last-ditch wish.

I showed up at Gacy's, and what happened sounds so preordained now as I compromise my secret self enough to type it—I immediately fell out of what I'd thought was love with Piest, not that I had ever been, and the idea of having sex with him seemed weird and morbid. I weighed what options I had left, then let him die horribly and let Gacy spot a light bulb, say, "Light," go to prison, and be executed in peace. In other words, I barely wished.

Then I finally turned my wishes loose on people in my life or on its periphery and went straight for love. Sex too, but that was only like a set of stairs I climbed to get where I was going. I picked on guys who were available to varying degrees, and wishing gradually became a kind of technical exercise that rendered every person doctoring within it so interchangeably ideal that no one recognized me anymore, or I them.

The problem, or perhaps the worst of many problems,

was that the love my imagination had constructed as an endpoint wasn't getable through simple back-and-forths, even with neurotics. My wish had started at the top by wanting death to love me. I'm talking totally absorb me, mysteriously and without rewards, ending every other thing besides itself, a love so violent that even John Wayne Gacy's victims were like bricks laid out before a bricklayer.

Eventually, I stopped wishing altogether, except for normal shit like money. I never used George in a wish again, even though, in retrospect, he was so unknowable, such a blur, someone whose love was so difficult to imagine manifesting, that fantasizing love from him would decimate me might have worked, whatever I thought "worked" meant. We stayed real guys, dealing with the tumult of his mental illness, and waiting for it to go away or kill him.

I still dreamed of reinventing George but only in the safety of my writing, poems and terrible short stories at that point, and later novels, five of them, where I tried to recapitulate him, make him sexier, or semi-sane, or so cute his insides didn't matter, sometimes by name, sometimes renamed and given similar but hotter bodies, other talents, different issues, and you can find out how terribly he fared in every variation if you want: George,

David, Kevin, Ziggy, Robin, Chris, Drew, Sniffles, Egore, Dagger, George.

I wrote the books thinking George would read the Cycle and go, "Wow, you think I have so many possibilities, you find me so inspiring, you wanted me to die young so much more spectacularly than the boring way I wanted to, you must love me, I mean you'd have to, and I must love you too, how could I not after all the work you've done, and I do," but he killed himself before the first of them was even published.

When George was 18, he found a useful medication. It merged the half of him who couldn't stop fidgeting and saying everything that crossed his mind at frantic speed with the other half who lay in bed and stared. He became as close to a complete George as he would ever be, and it was sort of possible to think that very strange guy was George and not just an experimental composition caused when both conflicting measures were being played at once.

Even that shaky George seemed a kind of miracle to me, and to him too for as long as that medication worked and while he lasted. And what I mostly would have wished from him happened, like for real. Some defect of the medication spun his mania into a sex addiction, and we had sex like we were wrestling each

other for a knife, and our exhausted cuddling afterward would feel like love, to me at least, sometimes
for hours.

The pill worked until his middle-20s. Then he tore
apart again. We tried to edit ourselves back into friends,
which we'd never really been. Being "put up with" at
that age was too dark for George. He stopped talking to
me. I moved away, so far away that I didn't have a phone
in my apartment. My letters to him bounced. I thought
or wished another pill had eventually unified him. It was
only years after he was dead that I was wrong.

George worsened. After three involuntary psych holds,
he quit pretending he was sane. He threatened to kill
a girl he didn't love but wanted to be loved by and was
arrested. He had to move in with his parents, and I
guess, or can only think, having known him as well as
anybody had, that he knew by then or thought he knew
that he would never stop exploding under wraps, and
there was no wrap left anyway.

In January 1987, George took an overdose of pills
that didn't work. Two days after being checked out
of the hospital he tried to kill himself by totaling his
father's car, but he survived. At that point, his family
gave up on him. He bought a gun and hid it for a few
days. On his 30th birthday, he blew his brains out in his

bedroom while listening to Nick Drake singing sadly to him about what he thought he heard as death.

You can make a movie based on *Peter Pan* and cast a pretty boy who has the minimum amount of talent needed, but he can never be more than the buffer or the life raft of the famous illustrations that deformed the story and preconfigured the appearance of their actor. Drawings can only hope to nail a character's resemblance, and they're just distractions from whatever wish was dying in the writer when he typed it.

THE CRATER

At 3 A.M., or whatever time it happens, life in San Marino, California, isn't much, but it's what it is.

A gun fires in a house, and now it's something for them.

Others in the house, mother, brother, are roughly woken up. They think about the sound, recognize it, and that's that.

It's the least surprise ever. Or not it, or that it happened, or with a gun, or that they had to hear it, or why now, but why.

The brother, now awake, now just the brother, stands before the noisy door. He hears Nick Drake. He says, "George," loud enough to penetrate the door and Drake, but it's not a question.

His mother is behind him down the hall, he can feel it, but he's too shocked to turn and say, "Don't come."

What do they feel? I don't know, but it must be very ugly since so much of it is hatred.

The door is locked. "George . . . George . . . George."

George is, I don't know, sitting, slumped forward. Blood is pouring from his mouth and nose. I was told that. There's a crater in his head. The top back part. It's full of mangled brains and skull and blood. He fired into his mouth, I was told, and so it would have to be there.

The crater can't talk or do anything. It needs an artist.

The brother kicks the door in. The room's very small, and he sees what I described. What I described will be the only thing he ever sees when he remembers George beginning now and more resolutely once he has to make a choice between looking at a box of ashes on his mother's mantlepiece or remembering this. This will be like George's album cover.

"Don't, Mom, don't," he says.

Someone calls Emergency, and let's say a vehicle arrives. Two men in uniforms get out, both men since women weren't thought capable of transcending this much trauma in the '80s. They enter the house. One is older, tough. The other's young and took the job for different reasons.

They're shown George's body and hate it.

The young one, Joe, let's say, is the one who has to do things around the body, and the older one, named something else, who cares, is the one who has to go into the living room and ask the family questions and then use their phone to call in a report.

"How old," the older one asks.

"Thirty," George's mother says. "It's his birthday."

You can guess the rest.

In two days, George will be ashes. He'll weigh 4.7 pounds. There'll be a funeral to which almost no one is invited—the estranged father, stoners from the park that George had started hanging out with, people who'd been kids when George was and haven't seen him since. They won't invite me. They could call my mother's house and try to reach me, but they won't. Nick Drake won't be played. There'll be no obituary in the local paper. No one in the family will want to write it. They'll redo the room, sell the house, move. They won't tell the newer owners. They'll just erase an awful, sick, depressing man.

Joe is in the room doing things he is assigned to do. He looks at the body from different angles, in detail, up close, at the bloody face, at the bloody floor, at the gun, at the hand it's resting on, always writing notes or checking boxes on a form clamped to a clipboard.

He keeps looking at the crater, he can't help it. He has no feelings that he knows of, and the wound is fascinating to him even though it's what it is and there is nothing to write down about it.

"Why are you so interested?" asks the crater. The voice is male, like the body would have had, but not as hued as you'd expect the voice of someone who would do that to himself to be, and the crater doesn't move in sync with it or even shiver like a woofer.

Joe is startled, but he's always startled when something like that happens. Death is so unknown.

"I'm an artist," he says. "I look at everything artistically. It's easier that way."

"I was an artist too," the crater says. "Or I tried to be."

"What kind?" Joe asks.

"My body played guitar," the crater says.

Joe goes back to doing what he's told to do. The crater has gone silent for a while, so maybe it has died.

"You there?" Joe asks it.

"Thinking," the crater says.

"About what?" Joe asks.

"A friend," the crater says.

"A good friend?" Joe asks.

"Yes, but not good enough," the crater says.

FINALE (1976)

I worship the ground he walks on. I wish there was a way for me to let you know that cliché was blurted into language, that an impulse I could not control just grabbed those words to get it out.

I wish I could type something that would immediately detail my love's massive extent and indicate what love's crippling effect on language has reduced or enlarged me to.

It definitely feels like I'm enlarged, but my thing for language hasn't come along yet. I'm too in love with him to talk coherently about it.

I love him so much that I'm nothing but that. Everything else I feel and do is like a habit or a doomed revolution.

I would literally declare everywhere he steps to be a sacred site by means and powers I don't know or have if there wasn't so much trodden ground already, and if I owned the footsteps' rights and weren't so busily in love with all the rest of him.

If he stood somewhere long enough to leave an imprint of his shoes, and if I saw the dents, I would want to hire an architect to do something visionary with them until I thought about a greater and even less constructive way to honor him.

Reality is so controlling, and I've never tried to stay there when I write before. This is the first time in my life that someone in the world has made me want to undermine my fiction when it frees me to forget the world and to seduce or fuck or murder or be loved by him or anyone I want.

I've never written fiction like I think and talk and feel before. I'm not sure why I believe that being willfully vulnerable and the verbiage that might result are a tribute to him or why I'm willing to bet this will talk to you.

It's a lot to ask since what I feel is not something I can capture, other than to say, Look, I'm another writer who is obviously in love and who has lost my way linguistically. How do I make you care, since no one cares that much about another's love.

I want to use my love as a perspective that will turn my writing into his devotee and insider and turn you into his, I don't know, admirers maybe. At the same time, I'm writing this for him, to him, no one else, and you're my, I don't know, imaginary witnesses.

You want literary kicks, and I realize that for you he's circumstantial. He'll work for you or won't. You're there to be convinced and help me prove my love is not meaningless to him. If I can sway you, and if he thinks I did, he'll know how incredibly I love him, if that matters to him, and if he doesn't know already.

This is a novel that only wants to really, really matter to him in the hope that, if it does, that'll mean he loves me too because he'll know I could do anything I want right now, and I wrote this.

I worship the flowing lava and whatever else a billion years ago that eventually formed the ground he walks on.

ACKNOWLEDGMENTS

Dennis Cooper is very grateful to Carrie Kania, Mark Doten, Kier Cooke Sandvik, Gisele Vienne, Michael Salerno, Frederick Boyer, Jurgen Lagger, and Jeremy Davies.